S0-DZB-895

Paula Rinehart

One of a
Kind

· ·

A Kids' Bible Study About Peter

NAVPRESS ◑
A MINISTRY OF THE NAVIGATORS
P.O. BOX 35001, COLORADO SPRINGS, COLORADO 80935

The Navigators is an international Christian
organization. Jesus Christ gave His followers the Great Commission to go and make
disciples (Matthew 28:19). The aim of The
Navigators is to help fulfill that commission by
multiplying laborers for Christ in every nation.

NavPress is the publishing ministry of The
Navigators. NavPress publications are tools
to help Christians grow. Although publications alone cannot make disciples or change
lives, they can help believers learn biblical
discipleship, and apply what they learn to their
lives and ministries.

Third printing, 1992

Stickers: Kathy McCarthy
Cartoons: Keith Alexander
Cover and all other illustrations: Fred Harsh

A Scripture quotation in this publication is
from *The Living Bible* (TLB), copyright 1971 by
Tyndale House Publishers, Wheaton, IL. Used
by permission.

Printed in the United States of America

FOR A FREE CATALOG OF
NAVPRESS BOOKS & BIBLE STUDIES,
CALL TOLL FREE 800-366-7788 (USA)
or 1-416-499-4615 (CANADA)

Contents
. . . . . .

Author

When Paula Rinehart taught at Pantego Christian
Academy in Arlington, Texas, one observation startled her:
as she read and discussed the Bible with her students, she
found that they "taught" her almost as much as she taught
them. Paula decided that someday she wanted to write a
Bible study that would help boys and girls feel confident
that they could read and understand the Bible *for
themselves.*

Before she could do that, two exciting events hap-
pened. Paula and her husband, Stacy, had two children.
Now Allison and Brady are the ages of the children that
Paula taught.

In addition to *One of a Kind,* Paula has also written
two books with her husband—*Choices: Finding God's Way in
Dating, Sex, Singleness, and Marriage* (NavPress, 1982) and
Living for What Really Matters (NavPress, 1986). She has
been an editor for NavPress in Colorado Springs.

Acknowledgments

. . . .

I'd like to thank the children and staff at Colorado Springs Christian School for their help and encouragement in field-testing these Bible studies for kids. They were great!

A Note to Parents and Teachers

This study can be fun to do with your child or a group of children. And it's important that it be fun. Even if you do this study in a classroom, it shouldn't feel like another class. This is the Sesame Street generation. As someone has well said, "It's a sin to bore a child with the Word of God."

This study is the perfect thing to combine with a date at McDonald's. Green, leafy trees in the park provide a great setting for this kind of talking. Depending on your child's temperament, you might want to rely more on reading and discussion and less on paper and pencil.

When you discuss a scene in the Bible, talk as though both of you were there. You were sitting on a hillside that overlooked a lake, watching Peter getting ready to step out of a boat and walk on water. Or maybe you watched Peter as he ran out of the courtyard, wiping burning tears off his hot, embarrassed face. You were *there*.

Expect some exciting things to happen when you open the Bible with a child. He might just tell you what's really on his mind. And even more exciting—he might share something fresh from that passage that you or I would never think of.

Don't Get Stuck Using Your Stickers

You're not supposed to feel that reading the Bible is work. It does take a little bit of effort . . . but it's not supposed to feel like work!

That's why there are fun things like stickers in this book—so that you won't get confused and think you're in school!

When you see a triangle beside a question, turn to the back of your book and find the sticker with a *picture* that is part of the answer to the question.

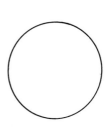

A circle means you should use a sticker when you find the one question in each chapter that asks you to read and consider a verse from a different part of the Bible. This verse will help to explain more about the passage you are already studying. That kind of verse is called a *cross-reference*.

Meet Peter
· · · · · · ·

Simon Peter was one of a kind. You would've liked him.
He had no secrets. Whatever Peter thought and felt, that's
what he did. He was the first disciple to boldly confess that
Jesus was the Messiah. And he was the only disciple who
later said publicly, "I never knew this Man." Some people
say that Peter must've had trouble walking—his feet were
often in his mouth.

Peter is all over the Gospels. He was just that kind of
guy. He talked when he should've been quiet. He ran away
when he should've stayed. He doubted when he should've
believed. But part of the reason why Peter is such a likable
guy is that there's a little bit of Peter in each of us. And we
know, when we read his story, that if God can change
Peter's life, God can change our lives, too. That's the way
God is.

Peter was quite a leader. Everyone followed him, even
when he went the wrong way. But when God really got
hold of his life, multitudes of people heard about Jesus
because of Peter. The world hasn't been the same since.

But here, let Peter tell his story for himself.

A Word from Peter
When I was a boy, I liked to bury my feet in the warm sand
as I walked along the edge of the Sea of Galilee. I used to
follow my dad down to the sea to help him get ready for a
night of fishing. After his boat was launched, I would stand
on the shore and skip stones across the glassy surface of
the water.

I was named after a famous high priest called Simon.
Lots of boys my age were named after this man. I had no
idea that some day my name, Simon Peter, would be better

known than the man I was named after.

When I was six I started school. Our school was called the "House of the Book," because the only book we studied was the Old Testament. Hour after hour, we sat cross-legged on the floor, swaying from side to side as we chanted long passages from the Scriptures in Hebrew.

At twelve, I was finished with school and I learned the trade of fishing from my father. Eventually, I owned my own fishing boat—in fact, many of the stories about me in the New Testament take place around this boat.

Just like my dad, I fished in the Sea of Galilee. This huge lake was known to be one of the richest fishing grounds in the world. People said that on some days the fish were packed so tightly that you couldn't throw a stone in the water without hitting several. We ate "fish and loaves" like you eat "hamburgers and French fries."

Let me give you an idea of what I looked like. I was a big guy with broad, strong shoulders and muscles that rippled up and down my back. Carrying heavy fishing nets was hard work! My face was leathery and tanned from the sun, and my skin was usually covered with a thin film of sweat and sea spray.

When I say that I was a Jew, that tells you a lot about me. The Jews were God's chosen people, but we had been beaten down and mistreated for centuries. Then we lived under the miserable rule of Rome. But as every Jew knew, the golden age was sure to come—when the one true God would rule the world and tread His enemies under His feet. I had grown up, like all other Jews, hoping that I would live to see the Kingdom that would last forever and to meet the promised King.

My brother, Andrew, met Jesus before I did. He recognized quickly that Jesus was the One we had all been waiting for. He ran home to get me. "We've found the Mes-

siah," Andrew told me, and he took me to meet Him, too. I think I had waited all my life for that moment.

After I met Jesus, fishing didn't seem like much fun anymore. I found myself following this Man wherever He went.

CHAPTER 1

Can a Carpenter Tell a Fisherman How to Fish?

P eter slowly lifted his tired legs over the side of his fishing boat, grateful to plant his feet on land again. What an exhausting night of fishing! For hours on end, he and James and John had let down their heavy fishing nets, first in one spot and then in another. They caught nothing but weeds.

As the morning sun warmed Peter's back, he found himself kicking at the sand in frustration. Yes, you could make a good living fishing in the Sea of Galilee—but not if you had many nights like this one.

Suddenly his ears heard a voice he immediately recognized. It was Jesus! Peter watched as Jesus made His way across the sand, teaching the crowd that followed Him as He walked. He looked at Peter and motioned him back to his boat.

"Let's take your boat out just a little, and I'll sit and teach from there," He said, knowing the water would carry His voice to the crowd on the shore.

Peter made himself comfortable and listened with the others, calmed and encouraged by what Jesus said. But then the Lord turned to him a second time, and this time His words startled Peter.

"Put out into the deep water and let down your nets for a catch," He said. Peter sat up with a jolt and shook himself awake. Had he drifted off to sleep? Was Jesus suggesting they fish in the morning light when every fish in the Sea of Galilee could see their nets?

Peter looked at Jesus again, studying His face. He knew the answer—yes, he'd heard Jesus right. Peter started immediately to search for the rope that held the anchor to his boat. But even as the boat began to move out into the calm morning water, he felt he had to remind the Lord, "Master, we worked all night and we caught nothing."

. . . .

Have you ever been so surprised that you almost dropped your teeth? That's what happened to Peter and his friends.

Follow them out into the water, as they once again put down their nets. Read the story in Luke 5:1-11.

 What clues can you find in verses 6-7 that show the men caught a lot of fish?

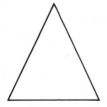

2 What do you think the other fishermen were saying to each other? (verse 9)

3 Jesus said that from now on they would be catching men. Did that mean they'd be hauling people around in nets? What *did* He mean?

4 When Peter and his friends got back to land, they must have put away their fishing gear like they never intended to use it again. Why do you think they did that?

5 Whenever a person decides to follow Jesus, it's because he or she is convinced that God offers something better. Everything else loses some of its shine.

a. Read Psalm 34:8 and write it in your own words.

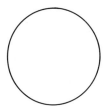

b. In what way does this verse promise "something better"?

6 What would change in your life if you said, as Peter and his friends did, "Following Jesus is the most important thing in my life"?

One big idea I got from this story was...

Quick Draw

In the empty box, draw whatever picture comes to your mind from Luke 5:6-9. Make the characters say whatever you think they would've said. ▼

CHAPTER 2

How Long Can You Tread Water?

"Ten, eleven, twelve, that's it!" Peter said, as he finished counting and straightened his aching back. Before him sat twelve full baskets of broken loaves of leftover bread. "What an amazing Man Jesus is," Peter thought. "I've seen Him feed over 5,000 people today from only five loaves and two fish!"

"Peter!" He turned suddenly as he heard Jesus call his name. "Take your boat with these men, and I'll go up on the mountain to pray while you cross over to the other side," Jesus told him.

As Peter and his friends readied the boat, they eyed some dark gray clouds in the western sky a little nervously. The wind was starting to pick up, too. And these fishermen knew how easily a casual wind could become a violent storm on the Sea of Galilee.

Every hour on the water was harder than the hour before. They had to row very hard against the strong wind. By the middle of the night, the waves were beating against the sides of the boat. Every few seconds another spray of cold water left Peter and his friends drenching wet. The wind whipped around his face, stinging his cheeks with wet strands of hair. How these men wished Jesus had come with them!

But wait. . . . Who and *what* was the figure walking toward them on the water? *On the water!* Some people said that ghosts lived in caves beside the lake, and now one was coming toward them! "It's a ghost!" they cried out in fear.

· ·

This is the way one of the most exciting stories in the New Testament begins. Read this story in Matthew 14:22-33 and imagine what it would have been like to be in Peter's boat that night.

1 Peter got over his fear quite quickly. How was he able to do that? (verses 25-27)

2 Think about what Peter did. How do you think he felt as he got ready to step over the side of the boat? Finish Peter's sentence: *As the waves splashed against the side of the boat, I put my foot over the edge and . . .*

3 In another scene on the stormy Sea of Galilee, Jesus spoke to the wind and waves and they immediately became still. On this night, do you think the sea became calm as Peter walked toward Jesus? Why or why not? (Verse 30 gives you a clue.)

4 Sometimes Jesus comes to us during a "storm" in our lives—a difficult time He wants to help us walk *through*.

a. Describe any sort of "storm" (difficulty, trouble, or disappointment) in your life right now.

b. How does Jesus want to help you walk through that storm?

5 Two men in history have walked on water—Jesus Christ *and* Peter. When and why did Peter start to sink? (verses 30-31)

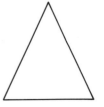

6 What happened when Jesus and Peter got into the boat? (verses 32-33)

7 When the Lord reached out and rescued Peter, he learned again how much God cared for him. Much later in Peter's life, he wrote about that care. What did Peter encourage us to do in 1 Peter 5:7?

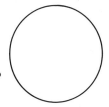

One big idea I got from this story was...

_____

_____

_____

Quick Draw

In the empty box, draw whatever picture comes to your mind from Matthew 14:27-31. Make the characters say whatever you think they would've said. ▼

CHAPTER 3
Do Strong Guys Ever Cry?

The night air hung like a heavy blanket over the Garden of Gethsemane. Peter was losing the struggle to keep himself awake. He drifted in and out of sleep. But he was always aware of the lone figure of Jesus only a few yards away. Even in his sleep, Peter could hear the deep groanings and the agony Jesus felt as He prayed.

Twice now Jesus had asked Peter to stay awake and pray with Him. Something bad was about to happen— Peter sensed it in the air. He knew that Jesus needed him, but his eyelids were so heavy that he drifted off to sleep again.

The next time Peter woke up, he was startled to see a crowd of men with swords and clubs in their hands moving toward them. Their torches set the night ablaze. They were coming for Jesus. Somehow, deep down, Peter knew this was the beginning of the end.

All of a sudden, Peter began to remember some of the words Jesus had spoken: "One of you will betray Me. . . . The Son of Man must be delivered up to death. . . ." Many times Jesus had said these words, but no one seemed to understand. Now, it all started to make sense.

Peter did the only thing he knew to do. He waited until the crowd of men came nearer, and then he grabbed his sword. If Jesus wasn't going to fight for Himself, well then Peter would.

Peter lifted his sword above the head of the high priest's slave, intending to slice the slave's head open. One quick blow and these men would know Peter meant business. Evidently he wasn't fully awake. He misjudged his target and cut off the man's ear instead!

. . . .

When Jesus was taken away by the mob, all His disciples, including Peter, fled.

Somehow, Peter and John managed to follow Jesus at a distance. John went into the room where Jesus' trial was taking place. But Peter stood outside with the officers and the servants.

Read Luke 22:54-62 to see what happened next.

1 Jesus had warned Peter about a hard time of testing and trial. Read Luke 22:31-34. What was Peter's confident reply to Jesus?

2 Peter was *sure* that he was equal to any challenge. He was so confident that he didn't even bother to pray. But Peter must have watched and heard terrible things happening to Jesus during the trial.

a. What does Matthew say was happening to Jesus? (Matthew 26:67-68)

b. How would Peter have felt as he watched and heard this? What might he have thought?

3 **a.** After Peter's last denial, he heard the rooster crow. Jesus looked right at him (Luke 22:60-61). How do you think Peter felt at that moment?

b. What did Peter do? (verse 62)

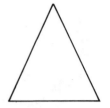

4 Think back over the opening story and the Scripture you've read. Add up all the ways you can remember that "confident" Peter failed Jesus—from the Garden of Gethsemane to the courtyard. How many failures can you remember? List them here.

5 From what you've read of Peter's story so far, why do you think he failed to remain loyal to Christ?

6 **a.** Can you remember a time when you failed someone—maybe your parents or a close friend—maybe even the Lord? What was that failure?

b. What have you learned from Peter's story that might help you avoid future failure?

7 Peter's story doesn't end with his bitter weeping. He learned from his failure. And later he wrote about what he learned. What does Peter say we should remember in our temptation and our failure? (1 Peter 5:8-10)

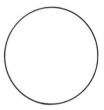

One big idea I got from this story was...

In the empty box, draw whatever picture comes to your mind from Luke 22:58-62. Make the characters say whatever you think they would've said. ▼

Quick Draw

CHAPTER 4
How Do You Start Over Again?

The first golden streaks of dawn were just beginning to light up the eastern sky. For Peter and
his friends, the morning couldn't come too soon.
What a hard night of fishing! For all their work,
their nets were empty. And so were their lives now that
Jesus no longer walked and talked with them every day.

The last of Peter's empty fishing nets dropped with a
thud on the deck's wet wooden boards. He sighed and sat
down in the stern of his boat. Somehow fishing just wasn't
the same without Jesus. Nothing seemed right about any-
thing now. Peter tried hard not to think of the future and
what he would do with his life. The future only reminded
him of the past and of how he had failed the Lord.

Peter was so lost in his despair that, at first, he didn't

even hear the vaguely familiar voice calling from the shore. "Friends," the Man on shore said, "you don't have any fish, do you?" This Man seemed to already know the answer to the question He asked.

"Put down your nets on the right-hand side of the boat and you will find a catch," the Man called out with confidence. What a strange request! Everyone knew that you fished from the left side of a boat. But, why not give it a try?

As soon as John saw the fish flopping in the nets, he realized this Man on the shore was no stranger. This was Jesus! John remembered how, only a few years ago, Jesus had filled their nets after another exhausting night of catching nothing. John leaned over then and said to Peter, "It is the Lord!"

Never mind his failure—never mind his future. Peter dived into the water to swim to where Jesus was. Jesus might not stay long. And Peter had missed Him.

. . . .

Have you ever been anxious to see someone but a little scared, too? That's how Peter must have felt as he swam toward Jesus.

Jesus had appeared two other times to His disciples in His risen body that week. But this scene records Peter's first personal conversation with Jesus after Peter had denied Him.

What would Jesus say? Would He scold Peter or ignore him or pretend that terrible scene hadn't happened? Would He tell Peter he was hopelessly unfit to follow Him?

Just as Jesus had served His friends their last supper together, now He spread a breakfast of fish and bread before them. Read what Jesus said to Peter in John 21:15-22.

1 When Jesus predicted Peter's denial of Him, over-confident Peter said that even if everyone else fell away, he would remain true to Christ (Matthew 26:33,

Mark 14:29). That's why, after He served breakfast, Jesus asked Peter if he still loved Him more than the other disciples. Peter was not so confident now.

a. What was Peter's answer? (Luke 21:15-17)

b. Why was Peter timid about saying how much he loved the Lord?

2 Three times Jesus asked Peter if he loved Him. And each time that He asked, Jesus said, "*Simon*, do you love Me?" The name Simon means "unreliable." Why do you think Jesus used that name for Peter in this scene?

3 Why was Peter hurt when Jesus asked him the same question the third time?

4 **a.** One way Jesus showed Peter that He forgave him and accepted him was by giving him a special job. What was that job? (verses 15-17)

b. Jesus wasn't telling Peter he was going to be feeding woolly animals on the side of a hill. What was Peter supposed to do?

5 Jesus told Peter that he would die a martyr's death. Peter hated to think that he would be the only one to suffer. "What about John? Does he get off easier than me?" Peter asked. Jesus never answered Peter's question.

How would you write Jesus' response in your own words? (verse 22)

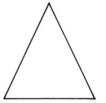

6 *Does God love you even when you fail?* An adult may assure you that God really does love you, but you must *experience* the answer to that question yourself. It has to be between you and God.

Read Psalm 103:8-13. No doubt Peter knew these verses and was comforted by them.

How great is the forgiveness God offers us, because of Jesus, for our failures?

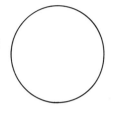

One big idea I got from this story was...

Draw a picture from John 21:18-22. Make the characters say whatever you think they would've said.

Quick Draw

▼

Going Fishing . . .

When Jesus first met Peter He spoke some strange and interesting words. "You are Simon," He said, "but you will be called Peter." Remember that Simon was a name that meant "unstable and unreliable," and the name Peter meant "solid like a rock." You can see the whole story of Peter's life in the difference between those two names. The old Simon would become the new Peter.

You've just studied four scenes from Peter's life *before* he really became like the name *Peter*. Take a few minutes to think about the way Peter acted in those four scenes. Would you have wanted him for a friend? If you'd been Jesus, would you have chosen him to be your disciple?

In the drawing below, decide which lines lead to the fishermen. Only the fish with the traits that describe Peter *before* the Holy Spirit changed him are connected all the way to a fishing pole and a fisherman. Circle those traits.

But wait. Peter's story continues, so keep reading. The man who stumbled his way through the Gospels is about to become the strong, bold leader God meant for him to be. Settle down and learn what God can do in someone's life.

CHAPTER 5
Can a Coward Become Courageous?

"Come on! If we're going, we'd better go now," John said to Peter. Peter promised to come back later and talk again with these men who were asking so many questions about Jesus. He ran to catch up with John as they hurried toward Herod's temple for the afternoon time of prayer. The temple was such a perfect place to tell their Jewish friends about Jesus.

Just as they were about to enter the gate called "Beautiful," Peter heard someone call his name. Everywhere he went, people recognized him as the leader of those who believed in Jesus—the One who had risen from the dead.

Peter looked through the crowd and spotted the man who had called his name. The man was crippled and had never walked. His friends were carrying him to the front of the temple, where every day he begged from people passing by for money to keep him alive.

As soon as Peter looked at the man, he cried out again. "Alms! Alms for the poor! Alms for the lame!"

Peter looked intently at this man, as though he saw no one else around him. *Yes*, Peter thought as he walked toward him, *what I have to give you is better than money.*

. . . .

Can you feel the spiritual electricity in the air? Only a few weeks before, Jesus Christ had been crucified. Then He rose from the grave! Now He was with the Father. His followers, with Peter as their leader, were on fire with the excitement of telling others about Christ.

Since the coming of the Holy Spirit on the day of Pentecost only a short time before, Peter was experiencing the power of God in his life in a way he'd never known.

Read the story in Acts 3:1-19 of what happened after Peter met this crippled man. You'll see for yourself some of the changes in Peter.

1　**a.** What did this crippled man expect from Peter?

b. What surprise did he receive?

44

2 This man's healing must have caused a lot of attention and commotion. Describe what the scene must have looked like. (verses 8-11)

3 When Peter saw the crowd that gathered, he began to speak to the people. He could have made everyone think *he* was a hero, but Peter didn't take the credit for this miracle.
How did Peter say this man received the strength to walk? (verse 16)

4 Peter wasn't afraid of what the people might think of him. Three times he told them about their sin. What three things did Peter say they'd done wrong? (verses 13-15)

5 What did Peter boldly tell these people they had to do? (verse 19)

6 Maybe you'd like to know how much of God's power is available to you in your life. Read Ephesians 3:20. What does this verse tell you?

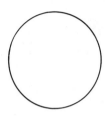

7 Maybe you haven't ever seen a crippled man walk or boldly told a crowd of people about the Lord. But in what other way have you seen that God is real and that His power is available to you?

One big idea I got from this story was...

Draw a picture from Acts 3:4-8. Make the characters say whatever you think they would've said. ▼

Quick Draw

CHAPTER 6
What Makes a Person Fearless?

"Tell us, by what power or in whose name have you made this man walk?" The temple priests glared at Peter and John, as if they dared them to mention Jesus' name.

Peter looked at the full circle of powerful, threatening faces that surrounded him. These were some of the same men who spit on Jesus and had Him beaten before they sent Him to the cross. Peter would've recognized those angry faces anywhere.

Now, though, there was the slightest hint of fear in their voices. They thought they'd dealt the death blow to the curious group who followed the Teacher, Jesus. After all, He was dead now—surely He was. They had watched Him die with their own eyes.

But they'd heard the talk that Jesus had risen from the dead. It was everywhere! And what's worse, as if proving the truth of that tale, Peter and John had gone all over Jerusalem preaching and healing the sick. People even brought their sick friends out on cots and laid them beside the road, believing that Peter's shadow could heal them.

The crowd listened for Peter's response to the temple priests. Who would he claim had healed this man who had never walked? Peter took a deep breath. He felt God's strength welling up inside him as he began to speak.

"Rulers and elders," Peter said, "if we are on trial today because we helped a lame man, then let me tell you this: By the name of Jesus Christ, the One you crucified but God raised from the dead—by His name, this man stands before you in good health. And there is no other way, there is no other name than that of Jesus by which you can be saved."

. . . .

Bold, confident Peter had come a long way from the time when he said three times that he didn't even know Jesus!
Read this story in Acts 4:1-22, especially verses 13-22.

1 Peter and John, two fishermen, were talking to the "big shots" and they weren't afraid. How did the priests and religious leaders explain the confidence of these common men?

2 The religious leaders held a private meeting to decide what action to take. What did they tell Peter and John to do?

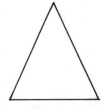

3 Remember, Peter was the disciple who had denied the Lord when a servant girl said he was a follower of Jesus! How did Peter respond now? (verses 19-20)

4 How do you think *Simon* Peter would have responded in his earlier days if he'd been threatened by the Jewish rulers? What might he have done? Pick one:

a. He might have clobbered them.
b. He might have run away.
c. He might have sworn he'd been mistaken for a twin brother.
d. All of the above.

5 Eventually, Peter and John *were* put in prison, beaten, and ordered again to be quiet about Jesus. Read Acts 5:41-42.

a. What was their attitude?

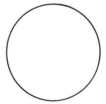

b. What did they do?

6 Has anyone ever given you a hard time for talking about Jesus? How did you feel?

7 What do you think makes a person want to keep telling others about the Lord *no matter what*?

One big idea I got from this story was...

_____

_____

_____

Quick Draw

Draw a picture from Acts 4:8-12. Make the characters say whatever you think they would've said.

▼

The New Peter

When Jesus first met Simon Peter He saw, as only God can see, both what Simon Peter was and what he could and would become. Simon did indeed become Peter.

The answers for the crossword puzzle below are words that describe what Peter was like after the Holy Spirit changed him. Have fun with it!

Down
1. Not weak
2. Someone who leads
4. Without fear
6. Saying the truth with confidence

Across
3. Calm, collected, and stable
5. A true friend is _ _ _ _ _.
7. Someone you can count on is _ _ _ _ _ _ _ _ _ _.

(Answers are listed on page 57.)

Peter's life answers a question that all of us ask, even if we never ask it out loud. This is the question we all ask: Can God change *my* life? In other words: Can He do something special through an ordinary person like me?

Now that you've gotten to know Simon Peter (the man he was and the man he became), how would you answer that question for your own life? What reasons do you have now for believing that God can change your life—that He can do something special *through you*?

The End of Peter's Story Is Not the End

Are you wondering what happened to Peter after his story ended in the book of Acts?

Peter became a missionary to the Jews in Asia Minor. He walked more than 3,000 miles telling people that their long-awaited Messiah had come—not yet as the conquering King they'd expected but as their suffering Savior.

Peter did become the spiritual shepherd that Jesus wanted him to be. Asia Minor (where Peter went) became the Christian corner of the Roman Empire. The churches planted in that area were the strongest of any at that time.

A man called Ignatius was a well-known Christian leader from that part of the world. It is said that, when he was taken to Rome to be killed by being thrown to the lions, multitudes of Christians lined the roads, waiting to receive his blessing and to encourage him. Many of those would have been people who had heard the gospel because of Peter.

Toward the end of Peter's life he returned to Rome. It was the most dangerous place he could have gone. The Roman emperor, Nero, was crazy. He had just burned Rome and blamed the destruction on the Christians. The whole city was up in arms. Every Christian was in danger. But Peter returned to Rome to encourage the Christians there. Peter the coward had become Peter the fearless leader.

Most people believe that Peter was crucified in Nero's garden as entertainment for his dinner guests. It is said that Peter asked to be crucified upside down, saying that he wasn't worthy to die in the same way as the Lord Jesus.

Next to the Apostle Paul, no other person had more effect on the early Christian church than Simon Peter.

Much of what we know about the Lord and how He works in our lives, we've learned through Peter's life and writings. You and I owe a lot to this fisherman who hung up his nets beside the Sea of Galilee to follow Jesus.

Answers for crossword puzzle on page 53.

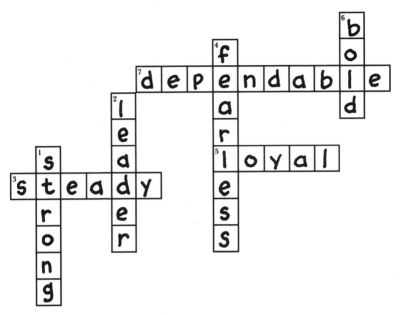